ORCA
YOUNG
READERS

The Undergardeners

D0026974

Desmond Anthony Ellis

ORCA BOOK PUBLISHERS

Library and Archives Canada Cataloguing in Publication

Ellis, Desmond Anthony, 1944-
The undergardeners / Desmond Anthony Ellis.

(Orca young readers)
ISBN 1-55143-410-5

I. Title. II. Series.

PS8609.L56U64 2006   jC813'.6   C2006-901020-X

First Published in the United States: 2006
Library of Congress Control Number: 2006922292

Summary: A boy called Mouse discovers
an incredible community beneath his backyard.

Free teachers' guide available. www.orcabook.com

Orca Book Publishers gratefully acknowledges the support
for its publishing programs provided by the following agencies:
the Government of Canada through the Book Publishing Industry
Development Program (BPIDP), the Canada Council for the Arts,
and the British Columbia Arts Council.

Typesetting and cover design by Lynn O'Rourke
Cover and interior illustrations by Esme Nichola Shilletto

In Canada:	**In the United States:**
Orca Book Publishers	Orca Book Publishers
www.orcabook.com	www.orcabook.com
Box 5626 Stn.B	PO Box 468
Victoria, BC Canada	Custer, WA USA
V8R 6S4	98240-0468

09 08 07 06 • 6 5 4 3 2 1
Printed and bound in Canada
Printed on 100% recycled paper.
Processed chlorine-free using vegetable based inks.

To Karen...

Acknowledgments

I am inordinately grateful to Maggie de Vries, who first read the story at Orca and went to bat for it. I would also like to thank Sarah Harvey for her considerate and considerable help in editing, polishing and generally improving the whole thing.

Chapter 1

Mouse lay in his bed wondering what had woken him up. His room was bright but colorless, the jealous moon having replaced the colors of the daylight world with many shades of gray. The dark hands of the white-faced clock on the table beside his shadowy bed pointed out that it was past midnight and time he was asleep, which he had been until something woke him. The model airplanes that dangled from the ceiling circled slowly in the breeze from the open window as though waiting for clearance to land.

He was a bit sore from helping his father put up a new fence around the back garden; he knew it was his own fault for trying to prove—as he always did when he got the chance—that being small wasn't the same as being weak. Because of his size, he was called Mouse by just about everyone except his mother, and even she sometimes forgot to call him by the name she had given him. His size meant he was sometimes made fun of at school, but he'd learned to take it in good humor; the teasing only got worse if he looked upset. So what if he was small for his age? He was only nine and he wasn't finished growing yet. But maybe he'd take it a little easier with the fence-building tomorrow.

There was only one fencepost left to put up. Four had been positioned eight feet apart, and his father had been digging the fifth hole when the post-hole digger struck the rock. No matter how hard they tried, they couldn't shift that rock, and his father had finally given up. He had measured off six feet from the last post, driven a stick into the ground to mark the spot, mussed up Mouse's hair and said, "Let's call it a day."

Mouse closed his eyes, held his breath and listened to the darkness. There wasn't even a creak from the house, as though it too was holding its breath. He felt himself drifting off to sleep again. The bed felt soft and warm and...There it was again! He jackknifed upright. A voice! That's what had woken him—a voice. And it was coming from the garden.

"All clear. They've gone to six." The voice was crisp with authority and carried clearly on the still night air. Mouse reached the open window in two bounds—and gasped in surprise at what he saw. Tiny lights were gathered around the last hole he and his father had tried to dig. Maybe it was a trick of the moon-light, but the rock they hadn't been able to move now looked as though it was standing on its end. There was a faint glow from the hole below. Feeling a little uneasy, he wondered for a second if he should call his parents.

One of the tiny lights now began to arc through the air, each arc accompanied by a strange voice. "Hun. Hoo. Hee. Hoar. Hive. Hix."

The crisp voice he had heard first asked, "Are you sure?"

The strange voice grunted in reply, "Hov hoarse h'yme shure." What on earth…? All thoughts of calling for his parents disappeared.

"Double-check the distance, please," the crisp voice said. "We have to be certain it won't interfere with the air-shaft. Now hop to it."

The light began its bounding flight back in the direction from which it had come, making the same strange sounds as before, but in reverse order this time. "Hix, hive, hoar, hee, hoo, hun." Mouse stared; the lights clustered around the hole were tiny lanterns carried by several small creatures. And whatever was making the strange sounds was hopping along on all fours with one of the lanterns between its teeth. I'm dreaming, he thought. That's it. I'm still asleep and I'm dreaming about weird goings-on in my garden.

Just then there was a horrified scream."Look out!"

The lanterns scattered in all directions, making streaks of light through the darkness as they went. One lantern hesitated, did a rapid zigzag back to its starting place, hesitated again and shot off in another direction. It halted almost immediately and a pathetic wail rang out. "Save me!" Thrown away in panic, the lantern flew up into the air.

Mouse was enjoying this dream. He rested his elbows on the windowsill and watched the light travel up, up, twirling end over end as it rose higher and higher. For one magic moment it hung suspended in mid-air before it slowly started down again, gathering speed as it fell. Down, down it came and then—an instant before it made contact—it illuminated a tiny head.

Ouch, thought Mouse. Then he let out a gasp. In the light from the falling lantern he had seen what was causing the panic in the garden. Without hesitation, he raced out of his bedroom, down the stairs and out into the garden.

Chapter 2

The grass felt very un-dreamlike to Mouse; it was damp and cold beneath his bare feet. And there was definitely something quite substantial about the low shrub which grabbed him by the ankle and brought him crashing to the ground. That should wake me up, he told himself. Then he thought how idiotic that was. If I'm dreaming, I haven't really tripped; I've just dreamed I've tripped. The blood that trickled from his cut ankle looked real, though. That is, it looked black, which is how he thought blood should look in the monochromatic moonlight. But he didn't have time to puzzle over it now.

"Mrs. Rochester! Beat it!" he called out to his neighbors' cat as he picked himself up. Mrs. Rochester was towering over the tiny man who Mouse had seen being hit by the falling lantern. Pinning his jacket to the ground with a sharp claw, the cat viewed him first from one side, then the other, as the little fellow lay huddled in terror.

"Leave him alone," Mouse ordered sharply.

"Whreoww?" said Mrs. Rochester.

"Yes, now, you big bully," said Mouse sternly. Whimpering noises were coming from her captive, who was trying to pull himself free of the daintily placed claw that held his jacket.

"She won't hurt you," Mouse consoled him. To the cat he said, "That's enough, Mrs. Rochester." Mrs. Rochester thought about it for a moment, then unhooked her claw. The little fellow staggered backward and fell flat at Mouse's feet. The cat swaggered off, her tail twitching imperiously in the air.

Mouse picked up the little man's hat, a woolen toque that could easily double as an egg-cozy. He held it out and watched the man clamber to his feet and begin to brush at himself in an attempt to remove the dirt and regain his dignity. The little fellow didn't come much higher than Mouse's knee. He wore dark trousers that buckled just below his knees over long stockings, and on his feet were stout leather shoes. A loose-fitting brown jacket over a dark shirt covered the upper part of his body. His large mustache with its curled-up ends was quivering rapidly, but whether from fear or indignation, Mouse couldn't tell.

With a rapid dart, the little man snatched his hat from Mouse's hand and ran. Mouse could hear what sounded like other little people running too. "Don't be afraid," he called out. "I won't harm you."

The sounds of escape stopped. Mouse heard whispering and, after a pause, the little man came back and gingerly approached him. "That was rude of me," he said in a gravelly voice. "I forgot to thank you. And I'm not afraid, certainly not, just cautious. I have seen humans before. We don't usually get this close, of course. And we certainly don't let them see us. We've learned that humans can be unpredictable. Especially when they haven't been properly trained. You have been, haven't you? Trained?"

"Trained?" said Mouse. "You don't train people. Animals are sometimes trained."

"Well I think a little training might do you all a lot of good. I suspect the only thing wrong with that animal who attacked me is that it picked up some bad habits from humans."

"Mrs. Rochester wouldn't have harmed you," said Mouse. "At least, I don't think so. I think she was just being curious."

"I'll bet she was curious." The little man jammed his toque back on his head. "Curious as to what I tasted like. And if slashing at me with those razor-sharp hooks isn't an attack, I don't know what is. But I forget my manners. Thank you very much for saving my life. My name is Qwolsh. Sole!"

The little man fell backward, only it wasn't so much a fall as a leap onto his hands, which he'd stretched out behind him. He kicked his feet in Mouse's direction, first one and then the other, before springing upright again. Mouse watched openmouthed. It was like watching a very energetic Russian folk dance. He could sense the other lantern bearers coming closer, but couldn't take his eyes off the little man called Qwolsh, who was standing again, hands on hips, gazing up at him. Mouse continued to stare. "Wh...wh...wh...what did you just do?" He managed to get the words out at last, his voice rising at the end of the sentence in astonishment.

"I thanked you for saving my life," replied Qwolsh. "And now we must be off. Just forget you ever saw us. Which won't be difficult because you'll never see us again. Farewell." Qwolsh saluted and he and the others began to move away, but Mouse took a step after them. This was his dream, after all, and he was going to keep control of it.

"Wait, wait," he said. "Why did you wave your feet in the air like that?"

Qwolsh stopped and said, "I soled you. Only being polite. Good manners after all."

This time Mouse made sure that his voice stayed steady. "Good manners?" he said, bending down for a better look. "I don't understand."

"The understanding of manners he doesn't have, at any rate. That, for you, is humans." The odd sentences were spoken in a low snuffly voice and sounded so close that a startled Mouse straightened up, stepped back, tripped over a small lantern and fell flat on his back. Close to his feet a voice said, "Ouch!"

Sounding as if its owner had a very bad head cold, the snuffly voice went on. "There you go, you yourself did it, though very clumsy you are."

"What did I do?" spluttered Mouse.

"Showed me your sole, you did. Now we've soled, you and I," said Qwolsh.

"Sold you what? I mean, showed you what?" Mouse felt this conversation was getting away from him, and he wasn't used to that; he was good at talking and rarely lost a debate at school. He got up and stood with Qwolsh in the glow of the circle of small lanterns.

"The soles of your feet," snuffled the head cold. "We show each other the soles of our feet in greeting. That's sole-ing."

"But that's silly," said Mouse.

"There is nothing silly about it," said Qwolsh.

"Most certainly not." A chorus of agreement went up from the circle of lanterns, and for the first time Mouse took a good look around him—and felt a moment's misgiving. His headlong rush out into the dark garden was uncharacteristic; he was more inclined to think things through very carefully before acting. And now he found himself in the middle of a strange group made up of several tiny people and numerous small animals. There was a mole with a pair of glasses perched on the end of its snout. A groundhog was holding a lantern between its jaws. Two mice held a miniature picnic basket between them. All of them stared at him with such an unafraid and curious intensity that Mouse felt a little uneasy.

He swallowed and continued. "Well, it's silly because...because...because you use all that energy just greeting each other, that's why. You could just shake hands, couldn't you?"

"Shake hands!" guffawed Qwolsh. "Now *that's* silly. What would we want to shake hands for?" He held both hands up and shook them from the wrist as though they were wet.

The snuffling voice, which Mouse now realized belonged to the mole, said, "And what about us who don't have hands, then?" The animal was standing on one hind paw, clutching a pair of eyeglasses in another. At the same time he was

14

scratching both sides of his neck with his front paws. "What about us, then?"

Mouse was confused. Paws couldn't be called hands, could they? "What I mean is...I didn't think...Most people, that is..." He stammered himself into silence.

A strong female voice called out. "Stop teasing the lad." Mouse recognized it as the voice he'd heard from his bedroom. The owner of this voice was the same size and dressed in similar fashion to Qwolsh; she had a satchel slung across her shoulder, and under her arm she carried a clipboard. "Our footing is very important where we live, below ground," she continued. "We show our surefootedness by touching toes." She gestured with the clipboard. "Qwolsh here was showing off a little by giving you a very formal greeting. Usually we just lift the other foot, like this, and touch the toes together." She lifted her foot in the air as she spoke. "Do it with me. I'm Alkus, by the way. Lift your other foot."

"What do you mean, my *other* foot? I haven't lifted either one yet!"

"Yes, I can see that. Lift the other one now."

"Look," said Mouse, politely but firmly, "how can I lift the other foot when I haven't lifted the first foot?"

Alkus gave him a puzzled stare. "The other foot *is* the first foot you lift."

Mouse was getting just a little bit exasperated. "You're making fun of me, aren't you? Just because I'm..." He stopped. He had been about to say "small"—but of course he wasn't small. Not here. Not now. Not compared to these folk. With a rush of pleasure he became aware that, for maybe the first time in his life, he was the biggest one in the group.

The mole's voice snuffled, "I don't believe the human knows his heart side from his other side; that's what I think." He nodded his head with such conviction that his glasses fell from the end of his snout.

"Oh, deary me," he said. "I've dropped my spectacles. Now where are my...?"

He sat back on his haunches and began to pat the front of the many-pocketed, sleeveless jacket he wore. He took a pair of glasses from one of the pockets only to put them back again, saying, "No good, reading spectacles." Then he took another pair from one of the other pockets. "No good, writing spectacles," he said as he put these back and found another pair in another pocket. "No good, working spectacles." He produced another pair. "No good, relaxing spectacles. Oh, deary, deary me. Ah! Here we are. Looking-for-spectacles spectacles." Placing these across his long snout, he began to search through the grass.

Chapter 3

"Is that it?" Mouse dragged his attention away from the mole and his many pairs of glasses and back to the problem at hand. Or rather, at foot.

Alkus prompted him again. "You don't know your heart side from your other side, is that what it is?"

"My heart side from my other side?" Mouse was puzzled. "Oh, I see what you mean," he said, suddenly comprehending. "You mean my left side from my right side."

"Ah," said Alkus. "What we call the other side and the heart side, you call the right side and the...what was it, the wrong side?"

"No," said Mouse, "the left side."

"Hy hoo hoo hall heh hah?" said the groundhog, the lantern hanging frim his jaws bobbing up and down as he spoke.

"Pardon me?" said Mouse.

"Hy hed, hy hoo...Ho hawhe." The groundhog flexed his jaw and continued. "Sorry. I forgot that was there."

"Was that you jumping about with the lantern in your mouth?" Mouse asked.

"That was me." The groundhog nodded. "I'm the people's ruler, you understand."

"I see," said Mouse. "And what were you doing with the lantern?"

"Lighting where I was ruling, wasn't I?" said the groundhog. "It can be danger-ous ruling in the dark. Light before you leap." He elaborated further when he saw Mouse's baffled look. "I was measuring the distances between the posts by leaps and bounds."

"So that's why you sounded so strange," said Mouse.

"I did not sound strange at all," said the groundhog.

"You did. You were making sounds like Hun-Hoo-Hee. Something like that."

"Nothing strange about it. That's how you would sound if you tried to count with a lantern between your teeth."

Mouse opened his mouth to reply, but decided instead to get back to his conversation with Alkus. "Anyway, what you call your heart side, I call my left side and..."

"Why?" snuffled the mole. Mouse saw that the animal was again balanced on one hind leg. And in each of his other—Mouse wasn't sure now if he should think of them as hands or feet or paws—was a pair of spectacles. The mole was rubbing all three pairs up and down on the front of his jacket at the same time. He stopped polishing briefly and again asked Mouse, "Well, why? And don't you know to gape is rude?"

Mouse realized that he had been staring open-mouthed at the mole. "Sorry," he said.

"Left side," the mole went on. "Why do you call the heart side the left side?"

"Ah, yes, left side!" Mouse said. "I call it that because...because..." he sputtered, "...because, it just *is*. Everybody calls it that."

"Oh, no, we don't," the group chanted in unison.

"Well, everybody I know does," said Mouse, a little more argumentatively than he intended.

"We call this side," Alkus said calmly, pointing with the clipboard, "the heart side, for the obvious reason that the heart is on that side. This side," she changed the position of the clipboard, "logically enough, we call the other side. So...want to try again with the other foot? Sole!" She raised her right foot.

Mouse took a step forward, narrowly missing Qwolsh's lantern where it lay on the grass. "Watch it! Watch it!" said a voice, but Mouse's concentration was all on this new ritual. He raised his right foot—his other foot—and touched his big toe against the toe of Alkus's tiny shoe. "Sole!" he said. Everyone applauded, and

Mouse felt a tugging at his pajama leg. Looking down he saw a little man who so far hadn't spoken.

"Why don't you join us?" asked the little man, rubbing the top of his round bald head as though polishing it. He was stooped and looked much older than the others and spoke with a voice that cracked with age. "It's time for our break," he said.

Everyone moved toward the end of the garden where, almost concealed by the dangling branches of a willow, a cloth was spread on the ground. A small picnic basket stood beside it. "Those helpers of yours are asleep on the job again, Glump," said Alkus, pointing to a lump under the middle of the cloth.

"Oh, yes, yes," wheezed the old man. "The youngsters of today don't want to work. Don't know what work is, most of 'em." He grabbed the edge of the cloth and pulled it smartly away, exposing the two mice huddled together in a ball, asleep. At the same time, the old man made such a realistic cat sound that Mouse was sure Mrs. Rochester was back. The two mice jumped into the air and came down clinging tightly to each other, their long ears alert, a single, entwined, quivering bundle of fur. They began to chatter in thin high voices, sharing their words and finishing each other's sentences. "What?"

"Where?"

"Did you...

...hear what I...

...heard just...

...now?"

The others laughed and Glump began to flick at them, matador fashion, with the cloth. "It's break time, you dozy dormice."

The mice looked around, their big eyes blinking suspiciously. Then they regained their composure, smiled at the company and said, "Ha! Ha!

...We weren't fooled.

Anyway, we aren't...

...dormice, we're...

...deer mice."

Glump chuckled and said, "Well, dear mice or cheap mice, you're dozy mice. Let's hop to it." Holding it by two corners, he billowed the cloth in the air. The deer mice jumped, caught a corner each and pulled it taut as it floated down. Next they each took a pair of long white gloves from the basket and pulled them on as Glump took leaf-wrapped parcels of food from the bag slung over his shoulder. Dancing back and forth, the deer mice began to lay the parcels daintily on the cloth.

"Glump is in charge of feeding us when we're out on a work detail. We came Uptop to get a closer look at the digging here," said Alkus, gesturing at the fenceposts. Mouse could see a pile of little tool bags on the ground beside one of the posts. "Those two," she added, nodding toward the deer mice, "are his helpers, Snick and Snock. Qwolsh you already know. This," she said, pointing to the groundhog, "is Chuck, and that," pointing to the mole, "is Digger." The groundhog nodded hello, but the mole was in a world of his own, polishing his spectacles.

"What's your name?" asked Alkus politely.

"Everybody calls me Mouse," said Mouse. All movement stopped. All eyes turned toward him, and he heard the disbelieving murmurs. "Because of my size," he added.

Snick and Snock chimed in. "Because of your...

...size? Those indoor mice must...

...be awfully big."

"No, it's just that, for my age, I'm quite small," explained Mouse.

Old Glump was at his side with a small steaming pot in his hands. He tugged at Mouse's pajama leg and said, "If we had mice as big as you down below, there'd be no room for the rest of us. Sit down."

Mouse was about to sit when he heard a reedy voice beneath him say, "Hey! Steady on. Watch where you're putting it."

"All right, all right," said Glump with

a note of impatience in his voice as he moved one of the little lanterns.

"Who are you talking to?" a puzzled Mouse inquired.

"Nobody. Nobody of the least importance," mumbled Chuck.

"Who are you calling unimportant, toots?" Mouse heard the reedy voice again but couldn't see its owner. It seemed to be coming from...But that was ridiculous. The lantern! It seemed to be coming from the lantern.

"That's an, er...interesting lamp," Mouse said tentatively. "What sort of fuel is in it?"

"Who are you calling a fool, knucklehead?" The voice definitely came from the lantern.

"I...I...I...di...di...di..." stammered Mouse. He tried again. "I didn't mean to offend. I'm very sorry. I had no idea that lanterns could talk."

"Oh, that's all right," said the lantern, changing its tone. "Apology accepted, apology accepted. And you're quite right, Mouse Mountain, lanterns don't talk."

"But you're talking, aren't you?"

"Yes I am, yes I am, yes I...am," trilled the lantern.

All the other lanterns took up the call. "Yes she is, yes she is, yes she...is." Their quivering voices climbed to a crescendo.

"It's not the lanterns that are talking, you see," the first lantern explained. "It's us, *in* the lanterns. We're fireflies. The prettiest and brightest things in the whole world."

The other fireflies loudly agreed. "Yes we are, yes we are, yes we...are."

"What a racket," moaned Glump. "Come on, you lot, your food is getting cold."

Mouse joined the others where they sat on the grass around the cloth. Everyone watched as he picked up the tin cup Glump had indicated he should use. "What a tiny little cup," he said, handling it delicately.

"You think that's tiny, do you?" said Glump gleefully. "What do you make of this, then?" He took his own cup from behind his back. It was so small that

Mouse would have needed a pair of tweezers to hold the handle. "I gave you the bucket," said the little man, and everyone exploded into laughter.

"Sorry if I was a little snappy with you earlier," said the firefly, "but the thing is, I have a short fuse." The firefly laughed uproariously at its own joke, sounding to Mouse like a bicycle with a squeaky back wheel.

Another of the fireflies added, "And she sometimes gets a little light-headed." Off they all went, a half-dozen squeaky back wheels. "Wheee-heee hcce-heee-heee!"

"That's enough out of you lot," said Glump. "Let's eat."

As they sat down, Mouse sipped at the concoction in the bucket that Glump had given him. It was quite pleasant—like very weak, very sweet tea. When they had finished eating, Alkus said, "That's it, we've done all we came for, it's time to go. Nice to meet you, Mouse Mountain. Sole." She held up her foot. Mouse touched it with his toe, but not happily; if he let them go, his dream would surely be over and he was enjoying it immensely. The doors of the lanterns opened and the fireflies flew out, dotting the garden with moving lights.

"Good night," everyone called to the scattering lights. "Till next time. Thanks."

"Not at all," bubbled the fireflies. "We were de-LIGHTED." And off they squeaked into the night in a ragged line, looking like a set of Christmas-tree lights that someone had flung into the air. "Wheee-heee-heee-heee-heee-heee!"

"Never fails," chuckled Alkus.

"Always the same...

...old jokes," said Snick and Snock, pulling off their white gloves and placing them in the basket. The others picked up their tool bags and headed for the upended stone.

"Alkus," Mouse blurted out. "Do you think it would be possible...? Could I...? I would love to see where you live. Could I come with you?" he finished in an excited rush.

Alkus looked at him for a moment. "I'm sorry, Mouse," she said. "Uptoppers don't know we're here and we want to keep it that way."

"Uptoppers?" questioned Mouse. "Is that what you call us?"

Alkus nodded. "That's our name for you who live up here in the harsh outdoors." Mouse didn't think the outdoors a bit harsh, except maybe in the dead of winter. He imagined living underground was harsher. "Your seeing us was unfortunate," continued Alkus. "I mean, it was fortunate for Qwolsh. But things would be better all round if you just forgot you'd ever met us."

"But I won't tell anyone," said Mouse pleadingly. "Please! I mean, I *have* met you—I already know you're here. So what harm would it do to see where you live?"

Snick and Snock each tugged one of Alkus's shoe buckles, and as she bent down they whispered to her, one into each ear. Stereo, thought Mouse, having a vision of Snick-and-Snock headphones.

Alkus nodded, then called the others into a huddle. Scraps of their conversation drifted toward Mouse.

"What if...I don't know whether...We've never had...Suppose he..."

From time to time one or another of them looked in his direction. At one point Digger gazed at him through three different pairs of spectacles in rapid succession. Finally Alkus turned round and said, "We've never taken an Uptopper below before, but you did come to Qwolsh's rescue, so you are welcome to visit." She sized him up with expert eyes. "If we stick to the main tunnels you should be able to fit without too much crouching." Then she said sternly, "But you must never tell another Uptopper about us. Promise?"

"Promise," vowed Mouse. "I'll never tell another Uptopper about any of the Undergardeners."

"Is that what you want to call us?" asked Alkus.

"Well, you do live under my garden," said Mouse.

Alkus laughed. "We live under many gardens. It's not what we call ourselves, but Undergardener has a nice ring to it."

"Well, come on then, let's get down there before the night is gone," said Glump impatiently, heading for the rock that had caused Mouse and his father so much grief. Mouse looked at the large pile of earth they had shifted in their futile attempt to move the rock. No wonder I'm stiff, he thought. Look at all that dirt.

One by one the Undergardeners stepped in. Mouse hesitated. The hole looked dark and uninviting. "Move along. We can't wait all night," Glump wheezed as he bumped into him from behind. Mouse looked around the familiar garden and then, taking a deep breath, he stepped gingerly into the hole. The Undergardeners hummed and the stone above Mouse's head began to lower itself into place, closing off the sky. The moon shrank to a half, to a quarter, to a sliver—then it was gone. With a firm *clunk*, the stone settled, plunging them all into total darkness.

Chapter 4

The steps were cold on Mouse's bare feet, and the air smelt musty. If this is a dream, he thought, it's a very realistic one. On the other hand, if it's not a dream, what am I doing here? Mind you, if it's not a dream, it's the most exciting thing that's ever happened to me. Wait till I tell... What am I saying? I promised not to tell anyone. His mood swung between cowardice and courage, dread and delight, as his thoughts chased each other frantically. If it's a dream I'm going to enjoy it. If it's not a dream...He took a deep decisive breath. I'm going to enjoy it even more. He swung his arm in a defiant gesture and struck something fleshy.

"Ouch!" The voice sounded like Qwolsh's. "Careful, or you'll put some-one's eye out."

"Sorry," Mouse apologized, stepped back and heard the deer mice scurry out of the way.

"And watch...

...where you're putting...

...your feet."

"Stand still," ordered Alkus, "till the lights come on."

The Undergardeners hummed and the darkness lessened slightly. Mouse began to make out their silhouettes. The place grew brighter and brighter. He could now make out the underside of the stone entrance and the stone steps that headed down into darkness.

"You did that with the humming?" asked an amazed Mouse.

"Did what?" said Alkus.

"The lights, the lights," answered Mouse.

"You sound like...

...the fireflies," chortled Snick and Snock. "De-lights!...

...De-lights!" They imitated the fluttery, high-pitched voices.

"If we was to leave it to the youngsters of today, we wouldn't even have lights," muttered Glump. "Don't want to learn nothing." He jabbed a finger in the direction of Snick and Snock as he went away down the steps, muttering to himself. "Not like in my day. We was happy to do whatever had to be done. No time off for floods and soggy muck. If it needed doing, it needed doing now. Real stick-in-the-muds we were and proud of it. Lost some of my best boots and tools in that same mud, but did that stop us? Never! On we squelched, bootless and toolless, man and ruddy, soggy boy till we dropped. We could habe dilor fast ald..." The words became unintelligible as Glump went farther down the steps until the darkness swallowed him.

"Glump does go on a bit sometimes," said Alkus. "Anyway, you wanted to know about the lights. We control them by humming at the required pitch."

Mouse was intrigued. "Could I try?" he asked.

"I don't think so, Mouse," Alkus said firmly. "The machinery here is very sensitive and its control is very precise. So just leave it to us, all right?"

"Pitch right, world bright—off by a fraction, end up in traction," said Qwolsh.

"Traction?" echoed Mouse.

Alkus explained, "It's just a saying we have. For safety's sake, you have to be very accurate. Many things down here are controlled by sound frequencies—the stone at the top of the steps, for example. Each is tuned to its own specific note, so..."

"Switch the pitch and you pitch a glitch," said Qwolsh.

They started down the steep flight of steps. There wasn't quite enough height for Mouse to stand up; he had to go down backward with his hands on the steps above for balance. He lost count of how many steps they had come down, but they were certainly well below ground level when they reached the bottom. More humming brought the lights up on a curved-walled, earthen tunnel stretching off into the distance. The tunnel was higher than Mouse expected, given the size of his companions; he had no trouble standing upright.

As they started along it, Alkus explained that many different-sized creatures traveled along the tunnels. "These are the main ones," she said. "There are others higher up that would be much too small for you. There are even bigger ones lower down."

The tunnel was very nearly round, and, standing in the center, Mouse could almost touch the walls on either side. The walls themselves were smooth, solidly packed earth.

Although he was paying great attention to his new surroundings, the operation of the lights was still in the back of his mind. It can't be that difficult, he thought. I bet I could do it. He let the others get ahead. "Humnnnnn." He closed his eyes and started to hum. He opened one eye, but nothing seemed to be happening to the lights.

"Who's doing that?" Alkus wanted to know.

Mouse didn't answer. Briefly there was silence, but then came an angry roar from close by, followed by other roars farther away. Openings appeared all along the tunnel walls as irate Undergardeners opened shutters and doors and popped their heads out, voices raised in anger.

"What is going on?"

"Who did that?"

"My dinner is ruined."

Every opening framed an indignant face as creatures of all sorts glared out into the passageway, many waving spoons adrip with whatever they had been stirring. There were little people, weasels and badgers and rabbits, skunks and mink, moles and voles and gophers and mice and many others Mouse couldn't name, all looking very angry indeed.

"Uh-oh!" Qwolsh clapped both hands to

his cheeks with a resounding smack that echoed off the walls. "You silly wantwit, you've shut down all their ovens, haven't you? Right in the middle of main-meal."

Mouse gulped and attempted to rectify his mistake by humming with all his might. Frantically, the others tried to stop him, Digger spluttering like a balloon from which the air was rapidly escaping.

"By my feet and inches," breathed Chuck.

"Now you've...

...gone and...

...done it!" squeaked Snick and Snock.

A distant wind approached, gathering force as it came. All along the tunnel walls, shutters and doors clattered as they opened and closed with the force of it. The dust began to swirl at their feet. Mouse stammered, "Wh...wh...what's going on? What have I done now?" He turned to Alkus in consternation, only to see a huge grin on her face.

"Never mind, lad," she laughed. "We can soon fix it."

"You've turned on the extractor fans, that's what you've done," shouted Qwolsh above the clamor.

"Full blast too," roared Alkus through her grin. With one hand she grabbed hold of Snick and with the other she caught Snock before the force of the gale blew the tiny deer mice down the tunnel. Supported by the wind, they now floated at the ends of Alkus's outstretched arms. Snock (or was it Snick?) had grabbed the picnic basket and Snick (or Snock) was clinging to the tablecloth, which quivered and snapped like a flag in a gale. The white gloves they had placed in the basket suddenly seemed to come alive. Stretching to attention, they leaped out and disappeared down the tunnel, tumbling under and over, flapping and slapping at each other in a mad glove dance. Above the screech of the wind, Mouse became aware of a humming sound. It was his companions humming for all they were worth.

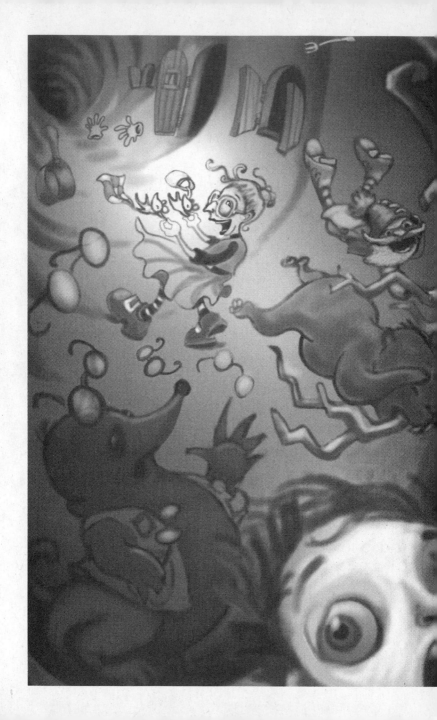

Gradually the noise diminished and the wind died away as they succeeded in bringing the hurricane under control.

"Wheeee!" squealed Snick and Snock as they floated back to the ground.

"That was...

...wonder...

...ful."

Mouse was horrified at what he had done. His mouth hung wide open and he was being very careful that no sound whatsoever came from it. Not so the mice, who were dancing around him, holding an end apiece of the tablecloth and chanting, "Do it...

...again, Mouse...

...do it...

...again."

"No! No! No! Do no such thing," growled Digger, who was scrambling about on all fours after his many pairs of spectacles

Chuck slowly raised his head from the earth floor where he had been holding on to a tree root with his teeth. Opening his eyes, he shook his head from side to side, saying to no one in particular, "Wow! What a...pthoo!..." He spat out some root, "...wind. Strongest we've ever had." He started making notes in a small, battered-looking notebook from his tool bag. "The sum of the roots...pthoo!..." He spat out some more root. "...No! I mean the velocity. The sum of the velocity multiplied by the centrifugal force added to the direction of airflow minus two feet equals...equals..." Clearing his throat importantly, he stroked his chin. Finally he snapped the notebook shut. "Well, well," he said weightily, "that was some wind." He looked down modestly as everyone murmured respectfully.

Digger, putting away the last of his many pairs of spectacles, said, "Very impressive, very impressive."

"What do you mean?" said Mouse, who liked things to be logical. "Minus two feet? Feet don't have anything to do with it."

"Of course they don't, that's why I'm subtracting them." The groundhog looked condescendingly at Mouse.

"Yes, but..." started Mouse.

"Thank you, Chuck," said Alkus. "You have explained it very well indeed. I had no idea it had such force." She tugged on Mouse's sleeve, gestured for him to bend down and whispered, "Don't make him angry. We have enough anger to deal with at the moment."

Mouse could see what she meant. The wind had made quite a mess; pots, pans, chairs, papers, mugs and plates were all over the ground. And the owners of all this rearranged domesticity were now beginning to mutter sullenly as they took in the extent of the damage.

One gray-whiskered weasel was sitting in the middle of the tunnel with a bewildered look on his face, his spectacles dangling from one ear. "What...Who...Where...Why..." His head jerked from one side to the other with each word as he sought some explanation for his undignified situation. His spectacles swung back and forth with each turn of his head, making him look like an old clock that couldn't make up its mind what time to strike.

"Evening, Mr. Glissomely," said Alkus. "Here! Let me give you a hand." She helped the weasel to his feet. The poor old creature was still muttering to himself in a bemused fashion as Alkus guided him through the doorway of his home.

The weasel was no sooner out of the way than Qwolsh shouted, "Look out!" Mouse jumped to one side just as a ball of wool went hurtling past. A large ball of wool. A large babbling ball of wool. Babbling? Screaming was more like it.

"Help!" came a frantic cry as it rocketed by. "Let me go!" The ball careered from side to side, swinging halfway up each curved wall of the tunnel like a skateboarder in a storm drain. When it came to the bend, it was going so fast that it looped right up across the roof and down the other side screaming, "Aghhh! Let me out! I'm going to be siiickkkk..." The sound trailed off as the projectile zoomed around the corner.

"What was that?" asked an astonished Mouse.

"I've never seen anything like it in my life," said Alkus, shaking her head.

"Whatever it was, it stole my notebook. After it!" shouted Chuck. "Come back, you woolly gangster." Chuck went bounding in pursuit.

"Come along, Mouse," said Alkus. "Let's get out of here before these good folks come to their senses." The residents of the tunnel were slowly returning to normal as the shock of the underground hurricane started to wear off and they began to recover their wits, their voices—and their dishes.

"What under the earth..."

"Does anybody know..."

"How is a body supposed to eat this soggy mess?" The voices sounded none too pleased.

Alkus spoke up. "Nothing to worry about, folks. Just some new Uptop machinery oscillating at our frequency. A little modulation on our part will solve the problem. We're going to deal with it right now." She led Mouse and his new friends away. "No need to let them know what really happened," she said when they were out of hearing. "They might not take too kindly to you. And they wouldn't be too pleased with us, either, for bringing you here. In future just leave the operation of the machinery to us, all right?"

Mouse was only too happy to agree. He gulped and nodded and said how sorry he was. Alkus continued, "All right, just make sure it doesn't happen again. Come on," she said to the others. "Let's get the kitchens operative again. Now what is that note?" she said, a look of concentration on her face. "I'd better check in the notes book."

She dipped into her shoulder bag and took out a shiny black and white book that looked like a cross between a tiny flat piano and an address book. Taking a stylus from the book's spine, she opened the book at the letter O. "Occupational, offices, openers, operations, ah, here we are, ovens." She ran the stylus down the list, and when she pressed on the black dot beside the word, the book piped a note which Alkus hummed. The others took it up and hummed along with her. After a moment Alkus seemed satisfied they had counteracted Mouse's sorry attempt at helpfulness. "Now," she said as she set off down the tunnel, "let's see if we can find out what that rolling cacophony was all about." Irate complaints of ruined meals and trashed homes faded behind them as they rounded the bend in pursuit of the bouncing, bellowing ball of wool.

Chapter 5

Before long they caught sight of the rotund figure of Chuck, who was following the ball of wool at a cautious distance. But if the groundhog was being cautious, not so the deer mice. They scampered alongside the rolling ball, following it up and down the walls like eager photographers in pursuit of a reluctant movie star. At one point they were running so fast they did a complete loop-the-loop over the top and met the ball of wool coming up the wall straight for them as they came down; it was only their speed and agility that saved them from becoming mashed mice.

Finally, with what sounded like a sigh of relief, the ball of wool came to rest. Digger changed his spectacles and peered at the wool with his face right up against it. He sniffed it, then gave it a nudge with the end of his snout. A sudden squeal from the ball startled the mole and he sprang backward. Snick and Snock scrambled hastily aside.

"Look...

...out, Dig...

...ger," they sang as they sprang.

Alkus walked curiously all around the now motionless ball. Snick and Snock linked arms and did a gleeful sort of Highland fling around it. The others stood aside and waited. They didn't have to wait long; after a quiet moment the ball of wool came to life again. "Would somebody please get me out of here?" a muffled voice implored from its center as it attempted to bounce up and down on the spot. "I don't know which end is up."

"Who's that in there?" asked Alkus, bending down close to it.

"I'm in here, you idiot," came the waspish retort. "Who's that out there asking who's that in here?"

"Alkus," said Alkus.

"Alkus," echoed the voice. "This is Soric. Don't just stand around out there like a fool. Do something."

"Soric! What under the earth happened to you?"

"Never mind what happened to me, just get me out of here."

Alkus hesitated. "Hold on a moment, Soric," she said. "If we let you out, you have to promise to behave. No flying off the handle and getting angry with everyone. Okay?"

"Just get me out of here!" came the furious reply.

"Do you promise?" asked Alkus firmly.

"Yes! Yes! I promise," the muffled voice snapped back. "Get on with it!"

"Very well," said Alkus, "let's see if we can find the end of this wool." They all began to search the tangled strands of the ball of wool, looking for a loose end.

Mouse was intrigued. He felt sorry for poor Soric, whoever he was. And, judging from the sounds coming from its center when they began rolling the ball backward and forward and from side to side looking for the end of the wool, so did Soric.

Chuck said, "I have an idea. Give it to me." Lying on his back, he got the others to hoist the grumbling ball onto his four paws, and when he had the balance right, he began spinning the ball with his feet. It gathered speed as Chuck's paws sped up until it was twirling rapidly in the air and the groundhog's paws were just a blur.

"Helllllp! Stopstopstop! Let me down," screamed Soric from the depths of his woolly prison. Chuck's notebook flew from the ball, narrowly missing Digger.

"You can stop now, Chuck," Alkus said. "You've loosened a strand."

Pointing to a tree root protruding from the roof, Qwolsh handed the loose end of the wool to the deer mice, who ran up

the wall and passed the wool through the loop made by the root. Then, laughing gleefully, they jumped and swung gently to earth at wool's end.

Arm over arm, all the Undergardeners now started to haul on the wool. Accompanied by many unhappy sounds from within, the ball began to bounce and twirl and shrink as it unraveled, until finally, there in the middle of the tunnel floor, lay a very bedraggled, dazed and dizzy little mouse-like creature. It had pale brown fur and a short, hair-covered tail, and it spat and hissed and bared its sharp teeth in a most pugnacious fashion. Shrugging off the last of its woolly bonds, it took a couple of staggering steps before getting its balance. Then it began to circle about in such a menacing manner that everyone moved gingerly out of its path.

"Now, Soric," reproved Alkus, "remember your promise? No fighting."

"Fight?" snarled the little creature. "Certainly! Singly? Or together? I don't mind. I can lick you all, every tunnel-digging one of you. Starting with those yappy little mice. What do they call themselves, Sick and Snack? I'll make a snack of them!" Prancing about in such a belligerent state, Soric wasn't looking where he was going and he smacked into Mouse's foot with such force that he knocked himself down. Jumping up ferociously, he stopped still when he became aware of the size of the foot. His gaze went from foot to ankle; from ankle to knee; from knee to waist; from waist to chest. As his gaze progressed, his expression became more and more incredulous until, by the time he was focused on Mouse's face, his own little face was almost all wide-open, staring eyes.

"Where are your manners?" asked Alkus, a huge grin on her face. "This is Mouse. Mouse, this is Soric the shrew."

"Mouse?" squeaked the shrew. He said it again, sounding even more astonished. "Mouse? Are you related to Sack and Sock? I was only joking, you know.

Actually I'm very fond of Slick and Slack. Oh, yes, indeed, some of my best friends are mice." The shrew's pugnaciousness seemed to have totally evaporated and he kept up a steady chatter as he slowly backed away.

"How under the earth did you manage to get inside the ball of wool?" Alkus asked.

"The ball of wool?" said Soric, his gaze fixed on Mouse. Reluctantly he gave Alkus his attention. "Oh, yes, the ball of wool. Well, I didn't know it was wool at the time, did I? I just saw what I thought was a worm flying past the end of my nest. I jumped out and grabbed it, didn't I? Next thing I knew, I was being blown along by this ferocious wind, wasn't I? I kept turning over and over and got entangled with the wool, didn't I? Before I knew where I was, I didn't know where I was, did I?"

By this time he had reached a turn in the tunnel and obviously felt safe. "I hate mice," he screamed back at them as he ran around the bend, waving his tiny fists in the air. "Always have, always will. Little wimpy things that just give rodents a bad name." But he had no sooner disappeared from view than he reappeared, bowing and scraping as he came, his manner having undergone another lightning change. "No, no, no. I like mice. Lovely creatures. Almost related, really. Oh, yes, as good as family. No. Better. Better than family. Especially Spick and Spock."

This extraordinary display got him through the bewildered group and as far as the bend at the other end of the tunnel. Then he was gone. All heads swiveled back to where the shrew had come from in time to see what looked like a small haystack moving their way.

Qwolsh shouted out gleefully, "Look who it is. Hello, Podge!"

"By my pins and needles," croaked the haystack, "has that yelping shrew run off?" As its spikes folded in on themselves, the haystack shrank and revealed itself to be a porcupine, who turned his head in their direction.

"Yes, he has. You scared him off, Podge," said Alkus.

"What a bad-tempered little beast he is," said Podge, turning around. "Had to put up m'quills to keep him off. By the way, you chaps, I'm lookin' for a...why, there it is!" he exclaimed as he caught sight of the tangle of wool.

"This wool yours is?" asked Digger.

"Well, no, not mine exactly. More Mrs. Podge's really," replied Podge. To Mouse's astonishment the porcupine had a monocle screwed into his left eye and a gaily colored scarf tied neatly around his neck. The ferocious quills were now almost hidden by black fur. Podge continued. "I was helpin' her, d'you see? I was lying back readin' a jolly good article about an experiment some rats had performed on humans. Most interestin', really. Apparently they got the humans to construct a maze and then they..." He looked up at Alkus with a puzzled air.

"I'm sorry," he mumbled. "What're we talkin' about?"

"How you helped...

...Mrs. Podge by...

...reading an...

...interesting...

...article," squeaked Snick and Snock.

"Oh, yes, of course," said Podge. "I was reading an...What was I reading, now?"

"Never mind. Just get on with it," snapped Chuck. The porcupine shook his head as though to straighten some parts inside and continued.

"Right. Well, anyway, Mrs. Podge was makin' use of m'hind legs to hold a coil of wool. I wasn't usin' em at the time, d'you see? When all of a sudden this roarin' gale gets up. Don't know where it came from. Haven't seen one like it since...since... oh, never mind, doesn't matter. Off goes Mrs. Podge's wool in the wind, d'you see? And off I goes along with it. Wasn't prepared, d'you see? Don't know how Mrs. Podge stayed put. Jabbed her knitting needles into the ground, I expect. Very resourceful,

Mrs. Podge." He shook himself and all his quill-tips moved in unison, like long grass in the wind.

"Anyway," he went on, "I managed to grab hold of a tree root and that stopped me flyin' about. Got a lot o' stuff stuck to me, though. Oh, yes, there are times when I think I'd be better off without m'quills. A porcupine learns early in life never to stand with his back to a strong wind. Ends up lookin' like a coughdrop that's been sucked and dropped in the dust."

Mouse was standing there open-mouthed, listening as the porcupine rambled on, knowing he was responsible for the poor animal's plight. "I'm really very sorry," he said when the porcupine stopped talking.

The animal now looked at Mouse and suddenly, quills aquiver, he sprang away, monocle flying from his eye. "By my pins and points!" he bellowed. "'Pon my peepers, it's a person. A boy-person by the look of it. Alkus, did you know about this?"

"Oh, yes," said Alkus. "We brought him down here."

"You did, did you? Jolly good," said the porcupine, walking around Mouse, his monocle dangling by its string. "By gollopers, he's a big 'un. Put up much of a struggle, did he?"

"Not at...

...all," squeaked the deer mice, sensing there was fun to be had.

"In on the capture, were you?" growled the porcupine, swinging his monocle by its cord. "Good fellows. Stout chaps! Never seen one this close-up. Fine specimen. Fine specimen."

"What do you mean, specimen?" said Mouse, not at all liking being spoken of as though he were an exhibit. "I'm not a specimen."

"Oh, fiery one, isn't he?" said Podge, stepping back further and looking up into Mouse's face. "Hmmn! Must be a good view from up there." His eyes glazed over and he went on absentmindedly, "Went up a skinny old pine tree once.

Quite a view. Dashed embarrassin', though. Couldn't turn round to climb back down, d'y'see? Fell down. My spines were out of alignment that day, I can tell you."

Alkus handed Podge an armful of wool. "No, Podge," she said patiently, "we didn't capture him. He is a friend who helped us Uptop. Saved Qwolsh here from a nasty scrape. We're showing him around."

"And you had better get back to Mrs. Podge with her wool before she has your quills for knitting needles," added Qwolsh fiercely, not liking to be reminded of his embarrassing meeting with the cat.

"Wool? No, no," said the porcupine. "She has lots of wool. I'd like to spend some time with this human." So saying, he threw the wool over his shoulder, where it got snagged on his quills. Jumping, he spun around and bellowed, "Agh! Monster! Get off, you brute. Off, before I quill you!" He spun this way and that, looking for his imagined attacker, until he became so entangled in the wool that he fell to the ground, a huffing, puffing, totally immobilized wool-wound warrior.

Digger's nasal voice came over the laughter of the others. He was sitting back, breathing with a hawing sound on the lenses of one of his many pairs of spectacles and polishing them with a cloth.

"Well, Podge," he snuffled as he wiped, "I think, haww"—he breathed heavily on the lenses—"that Mrs. Podge does a, haww"—he breathed on them again—"better job of knitting with only two needles than you do with all of, haww, your quills." He perched the freshly polished spectacles on the end of his snout and grinned.

"I can't hear you, Digger," said Podge, as the others helped him untangle. "You have the wrong spectacles on."

The mole looked confused and started to go through his many pockets, muttering to himself. "Must find my listening...Wait a minute! Ha! Ha! Very funny, very funny indeed. I can't hear you. You have the wrong spectacles on. Very good. Ha! Ha!"

"Showing him around, you say," Podge clapped his front paws and rubbed the palms together with a dry rustling sound; his quills bristled in a most alarming manner. "Right, then. What should he see?"

Chapter 6

The Undergardeners deliberated at length. Mouse fidgeted with impatience. Suggestions were made, discussed and dismissed. Fire Lake and the Invisible Mountain were rejected, as was the Blue Bagoo and the Green Gamee. Before they could discard the Ancient Rhymer, Mouse chimed in, "The Ancient Rhymer sounds interesting. Let's go there."

The Undergardeners looked at him in surprise, having quite forgotten he was there. "Right then," said Podge. "Are we off?" He screwed his monocle in firmly and sauntered off on all fours. Alkus winked at Mouse, folded her arms and waited. After several paces, Podge came to a stop and turned back with a puzzled look on his face. "Where are we goin'?" he said.

"You're the only one seems to be going anywhere," remarked Qwolsh.

"Yes, true enough, true enough," mumbled Podge. "Where am *I* goin', then?"

"We don't know, Podge," said Alkus. "But if you're looking for the Ancient Rhymer, you're going the wrong way."

Podge ambled back. "Really?" he said. "Could have sworn...Never mind."

Mouse asked what exactly an Ancient Rhymer was and what it did, and Alkus said, "It's a *him* and that *is* what he does. Rhymes! Makes verses all the time."

"Never stops. Everythin' has to rhyme, d'you see?" said Podge.

"He keeps a record of the happenings here," explained Alkus, "a sort of history. As well as supplying verses for special occasions."

"He wrote one...

...about us," squealed Snick and Snock and they began to recite the poem, taking a line each.

"Snick and Snock are very nice...

...Snock and Snick are mighty mice...

...Never mind how bad the weather...

...Both are always seen together...

...If you have reflexes quick...

...You can always pick out Snick...

...What a disappointing shock...

...To find it isn't Snick...

...It's Snock."

Gleefully they linked arms and danced enthusiastically to the words until they collapsed in a fit of giggling, which continued until Digger found his marching spectacles and the journey began. The deer mice each held a leg of Mouse's pajamas and skipped happily beside him as the procession made its way along the tunnel, with Mouse brushing aside the tendrils that dangled from the roof in places. He was so interested in his new surroundings that he wasn't watching the ground; his feet hit a tree root and he almost fell.

"Look out...

...Mouse Mountain...

...before you...

...flatten us," Snick and Snock screeched, dodging out of the way as Mouse, hands on the wall, regained his balance. Just in front of him, Podge's sharp quills quivered with each step the porcupine took, and Mouse decided to be more careful; he had no desire to fall on that lot.

Soon they arrived at an open space where many tunnels came together at a crossroads. A crosstunnels really, thought Mouse. An almost-bare signpost, its signs scattered in all directions, stood at the center of the clearing.

"I guess your storm made it this far, Mouse," said Alkus.

Mouse was embarrassed. "I'm very sorry," he said. "Can I put them back?"

"Don't worry about it," said Chuck. "It needed updating. My workers and I," he sniffed proudly, "have dug several more tunnels whose signs weren't even on the post yet."

69

Mouse picked up one of the signs. "Danger. Creepscreech's Lair," he read. "What's a Creepscreech?" he asked.

"Not a very nice character at all," said Qwolsh.

"Someone to avoid at all cost," said Alkus.

"Yes, indeed," echoed Digger as he rummaged through the signs on the ground. "At all cost to be avoided. This in a foreign language seems to be," he said, picking up one of the signs and holding it close to his face. Looks as though he's smelling it, not spelling it, thought Mouse.

"It's upside down, you daft mole," said Alkus good-naturedly. "It says 'The Ancient Rhymer,' and it used to point in that direction." She indicated a passageway with her clipboard.

"Sure about that, are you?" asked Podge. "I thought...never mind. Very good. Right behind you," he said, strolling ahead down the passageway. The others just shook their heads and followed. Digger fell in behind Mouse, muttering, "How odd. How very odd. Why would anybody want to paint a sign upside down?" In companionable silence, except for the chatter of the deer mice, they went on in single file until Mouse became aware of a faint voice in the distance, which got louder as they approached. The deep voice was speaking in a measured, sing-song manner, and Mouse felt sure they had reached their destination.

"Is that the Ancient Rhymer?" he asked.

"That's him," Alkus replied.

The ground beneath their feet was lit-tered with paper, and the pile got deeper the closer they got to the voice, which now seemed to be coming from just around the next corner. "Oh, my gosh," said Mouse, looking at the mess. "Did I do all this with the wind?"

"No," said Alkus. "I'm sure it didn't reach this far."

"Even if it did," said Chuck, "it wouldn't make any difference to the Rhymer. His cave is even worse."

"We were lost...

...for three days...

...in there...

...once," said Snick and Snock.

Mouse looked at the mess. There were sheets that had only one word on them. There were sheets torn neatly in half and sheets torn into many little pieces. There were sheets that were scribbled fiercely upon and sheets measled with inkblots. "Quiet now," whispered Alkus, holding up her hand as she reached the corner. "He doesn't like to be interrupted in the middle of a verse." Mouse stopped and there was an "Oof!" from Digger as the mole bumped into his leg and sat down heavily on an inky page. They all tiptoed forward and peered around the corner.

The cave of the Ancient Rhymer was dimly lit, but there was just enough light to see a most untidy jumble of papers. Piled to the roof in places, the swelling stacks went all the way to the barely visible corners. Papers overflowed from crates. Bags were crammed to bursting with them. Shelves sagged under many reams. Gasping tongues of paper stuck out from trunks so full they wouldn't close. There were narrow pathways through the jumble, and in the center of a small clear area, a little man stood at a paper-piled desk, bathed in the gentle glow of a single candle on a tortoiseshell candlestick. *On* the shell, not in the shell; the tortoise itself was in the shell. The candle was stuck on its back.

"I think I have it now, Sprint," the little man said to the tortoise, tossing the pile of papers in front of him into the air. The sheets made a sound like a flock of startled birds taking off as they flapped and fluttered upward before flurrying down again. Sprint, the tortoise, crawled under the desk to shield the candle from the paper's swirling fall.

The Ancient Rhymer had a big head crowned with an enormous mane of black hair. His ruffled shirt was open to

his waist, and around his neck he wore a large, gold medallion that gleamed against his chest. He had big bushy eyebrows that jiggled rapidly up and down in a most agitated fashion. Sometimes both eyebrows moved together, sometimes they moved independently, but at least one of them seemed to be in motion at all times. The Ancient Rhymer cleared his throat and started to move very slowly through the narrow walkways of the cave followed by Sprint, whose only job seemed to be to keep light on the page in the Rhymer's hand.

The Ancient Rhymer cleared his throat again, cupped his hand behind his ear and prepared to read, but at this point, unable to contain themselves any longer, Snick and Snock ran excitedly into the cave with cries of glee. This sudden commotion startled the tortoise, who reared up, dislodging the candle, which fell into the discarded paper. There was a *whoosh* and almost instantly the crisp dry paper was alight. The fire spread unbelievably swiftly. Mouse watched, horrified, as Snick and Snock, the Rhymer and the tortoise were enveloped in a cloud of billowing acrid smoke.

Chapter 7

Filling his lungs with air, Mouse dashed forward into the burning cave. Choking smoke engulfed him in an instant, going up his nose and making him sneeze. It filled his throat and made him cough. It made his eyes water so much that he had to squeeze them shut and feel his way along. "Where are you?" he called as he fumbled about in the murk.

He felt a tug at each pajama leg dragging him forward as two squeaky voices said, "We'll...

...guide...

...you."

Of course! Smoke rises. Down there, near the ground, it must still be fairly clear. "The tortoise and the Rhymer," Mouse shouted to the deer mice, "where are they?" As soon as he spoke, he found the tortoise—painfully. The big toe of his bare foot smashed against the upturned shell, making Mouse wince and sending the tortoise into a spin. He picked up the rotating reptile and tucked him under his arm. "Now the Rhymer," he gasped as he bent down and gulped a breath of the cleaner air near the ground.

The mice dragged him to where the little man was bumbling around, coughing. Mouse grabbed him by the collar and lifted him off the ground. "Okay, find the way, quickly," he called down to the deer mice. Mouse went where they pulled him, hoping they knew where they were going because he was completely disoriented and almost out of air.

To his great relief, the smoke began to lessen and they were soon free of the smothering clouds altogether. The deer mice let go of his pajamas and ran ahead, taking gasping drags of clean air into their little lungs. Spluttering and coughing, Mouse staggered a short distance from the cave before he put down his two passengers and wiped his smarting eyes on his sleeve. After a moment, his rasping breath eased and his eyes cleared. Smoke continued to pour from the Rhymer's cave. They'd have to do something about that fire. "Any water here?" Mouse asked Alkus breathlessly.

"No water." Alkus shook her head.

"Digger!" Mouse exclaimed as a solution occurred to him.

"Digger?" said Chuck.

"You want to throw Digger on the fire?" asked an incredulous Podge. "'Pon my word. What a novel idea." He ran his front paws one after the other down his long snout as though he was trying to make it even longer.

"No, no. Get him to throw earth on the flames by digging as fast as he can."

"Right!" said Alkus, flinging aside her shoulder bag. "Hop to it!"

"Super...

...dooper!" squealed the deer mice, with hardly a cough between them.

"Get him primed!" blared Podge.

The bewildered Mole was hoisted and carried face down and hind feet forward to the entrance of the Rhymer's cave. A trail of spectacles from his many pockets littered the ground in his wake as they hauled him into position.

"Dig!" ordered Alkus.

Digger began doing just that. His front paws scrabbled at the ground so rapidly that they were a blur as they shoveled the flame-smothering earth backward toward the fire. Everyone joined in now, flinging the loosened earth into the cave using hands, feet, Alkus's clipboard, pieces of planking—whatever they could find to smother the burning papers.

It was hard and sweaty work, but finally they succeeded; the flames died away and the smoke became a trickle. The fire was out. Puffing and panting, the smudged friends all smiled with relief and, when they got their breath back, let out a cheer that reverberated through the tunnel.

Then, "Hurray for Mouse," somebody shouted, and another cheer went up.

"Hurray for Snick and Snock," said Mouse, and they all cheered again. The deer mice looked at each other shyly, silent for once. Alkus chuckled and, reaching down, scratched the deer mice on the tops of their heads before she and Qwolsh went into the cave to check on the extent of the damage.

Mouse looked at those he had pulled from the smoke. The tortoise hadn't budged; he remained tucked inside his armored home, black holes where the legs and head should be. The Rhymer appeared to be totally unmoved by the danger he had been in. There was a faraway look in his eyes, and as Mouse watched him curiously, the huge eyebrows started to twitch and his lips began to move. Another poem, Mouse supposed. The Rhymer kept repeating the same line over and over. As if the verse he was trying to write was a car that would eventually start if it was pushed hard enough. "From the wise man's home came the billowing smoke...From the wise man's home came the billowing smoke...Came the billowing smoke. What rhymes with smoke?" the Rhymer asked of nobody in particular.

"Choke," said Mouse with a cough.

"Yes, yes indeed," nodded the Rhymer, throwing his head back and scratching beneath his chin to help himself think better. "Choke...Choke...Great wobbling wordsmiths!" he exclaimed as his gaze focused on Mouse. "Who under the earth...?" he stammered. "Wha...Wha... What a monster!"

"I'm not a monster," Mouse explained patiently. The novelty of his relative hugeness was beginning to wear off. In fact, he didn't think he'd mind too much the next time someone Uptop made fun of his size. "I'm an ordinary boy," he said. "Who just saved you from your burning cave," he added. He thought it was rude of the Rhymer not to have even said thanks.

The Rhymer's eyes and mouth opened wide and round. "Oh," he said. He had been so intent on his verse he hadn't thought about the fire. "My pens and papers. My desks and dictionaries and dabbled-in diaries. Everything ruined and burned and gone."

"I wouldn't worry too much about it," said Qwolsh, emerging from the cave combing his slightly sooty mustache with his fingers.

"Mostly smoke damage," said Alkus, following him. "We got to it in time, thanks to Mouse here. But let that be a lesson to you," she continued sternly, wiping her hands on a cloth. "You shouldn't be using candles. You have light."

She hummed and lights came on in the cave behind them. Then, looking up "Fans—extractor type" in her notes book, she hummed the given note and the smoke swirling around in the tunnel was rapidly whisked away. For a brief moment—a very brief moment—Mouse was tempted to join in.

The tortoise poked his head out from his shell and swung it from side to side, looking about him; craning his neck he peered around at his back, where Snick and Snock were perched as though he were a park bench. The Rhymer screwed up his eyes against the light and pulled his eyebrows down. From behind those woolly blinds he said, "Oh, no, no, no! Such mechanical light I have long eschewed. Bright light destroys the poet's mood."

"You nearly had more than your mood destroyed," said Qwolsh gruffly. "If it hadn't been for Mouse…"

"And," butted in Podge, "you haven't thanked him yet for saving your life."

Parting his eyebrows, the Rhymer peered upward. "You call this gigantic mound a mouse? Good gracious me! He's big as a house." Then he smiled. "But I thank you greatly for being so brave, and charging into the smoke-filled cave. And for saving me and my friend, he that Snick and Snock did upend." He gave the deer mice a fierce look and wagged a finger at them. The mice skittered away from the wagging finger and hid behind Mouse's legs as the Ancient Rhymer went back into his cave, followed by the others.

"Not at all," said Mouse. "I'm very glad I was here." With the benefit of the lighting, Mouse could see that the burned area didn't stretch very far; a small ring of charred paper marked the extent of it. But it's a good job we acted quickly, he thought. If it had all caught fire we'd never have been able to put it out, no matter how fast Digger had been able to dig.

Digger! Mouse looked around but he couldn't see the mole anywhere. "Where's Digger?" he asked.

"Whoops! Nobody told the silly fellow to stop," said Podge. They gathered around the hole in the ground. Of the mole himself there was no sign.

"My goodness me, he's gone," said Chuck. The mole's many pairs of spectacles were the only evidence that he'd ever been there.

"Digger...Stop," called Alkus through cupped hands as she stood at the mole-made rim. They could hear no sound from below. "Digger," she called again. No reply!

"He has...

...probably fallen...

...asleep," said Snick and Snock.

Qwolsh laughed and said, "Thought it was a new bedroom he was digging."

"Digger," Alkus called loudly into the hole. Her own voice echoing back was the only reply. "That's odd." She flashed a worried look at Chuck.

"I'll go down and see," said the ground-hog and he disappeared headfirst into the hole.

Alkus's tone had affected everybody. Even Snick and Snock were quiet. All waited in silence until the groundhog's worried face popped up again. His lower jaw wobbled up and down as he stammered out, "He...he...he..." Stopping, he swallowed and tried again. "He's g...g... gone." He got it out finally.

"Gone!" exclaimed Alkus. "How can he be gone?"

"I don't know," said the groundhog, sounding frightened.

"Nonsense! He can't have just vanished," said Podge.

"What's at the bottom of the hole?" Qwolsh wanted to know.

"Nothing." The groundhog's voice was so low they could hardly hear him.

"There must be something down there," reasoned Alkus. "It can't be just nothing!"

The groundhog said, "He dug down so far," he hesitated a moment, "that he fell through into a tunnel below this."

"We have no tunnel below this," said Alkus sharply.

"Exactly!" The groundhog nodded his head. "It's not one of ours. It must be..." He stopped suddenly and listened.

In alarm they looked toward the edge of the hole. They all heard it. It began as a dull rumble that got louder and louder until they found themselves stopping their ears against the noise. The ground around the hole shook, and Chuck scrambled from it just in time to avoid being sucked down. The irate creature below got a large dollop of earth kicked from the rim, and the Undergardeners heard a scream of anger as it clattered off, coughing and spluttering. Ashen-faced, they looked at each other as the awful realization sank in. Digger had fallen into the Creepscreech's lair.

Chapter 8

In stunned silence they stood around
the hole. There was a chance—it was
what they all hoped for—that the mole
was hiding somewhere safe. But perhaps
he was lying hurt from the fall and in
need of help. Or, most awful thought
of all, maybe he had already been dis-
covered by the Creepscreech and was
past help. Slowly, one after another, the
Undergardeners turned their heads and
looked up at Mouse. With mixed emotions
it dawned on him that he was the one
they were turning to for help. He'd never
been looked up to as a leader before. His
friends at school always expected him

to follow them. A warm glow ran though him. He liked this new role.

"What do you think, Mouse?" asked Alkus.

Mouse didn't know anything about this Creepscreech except that the Undergardeners were terrified of it. What did it look like? Was it big, small, fat, thin? What did it do to people it caught? Imprison them? Beat them? Eat them? What? "For a start," he said, "tell me a bit about the Creepscreech."

"Well, it's very..." began Qwolsh. He shook his head, pulled off his cap and began to chew the ends of his long mustache.

"It's rather more than that, d'you see," said Podge. "It's...It's..." Then he too faltered and turned to Alkus for help. She shook her head in consternation.

Chuck screwed up his face in a vain attempt to produce a solution. Snick and Snock made no pretence of thought at all; they just lifted a shoulder apiece in a blended shrug.

"Okay," Mouse asked next, "why does it hate you so much?"

"The truth is," Alkus admitted, "we don't really know much about it."

"But if that's the case," Mouse wanted to know, "how do you know it's an enemy? Perhaps it's friendly if you give it a chance."

"Ha!" snorted Qwolsh, his mustache bristling. "There are stories from the old days of those who ventured into its lair and were never seen again."

"You heard it yourself just now," said Alkus. "The way it came charging at us screaming and snorting—that didn't sound friendly, did it?"

"Broke into its lair once m'self by accident," said Podge. "I was digging a larder, d'you see? It must have been waitin', because next thing, it charged on the other side of the wall. Couldn't get to me, d'you see, hole was too small, but its foul breath came whistlin' through that hole like a hurricane. Twisted m'quills somethin' shockin'."

"Well, the first thing we should do is try to find out what happened to Digger," said Mouse. "What's it like down there, Chuck?"

"The tunnel slopes down at an angle of one-in-three," said Chuck professionally, "then suddenly goes straight down into blackness."

"Then we'll need a light, for a start," said Mouse.

Alkus scratched her head. "Bit of a problem, that. Our lighting system doesn't stretch to the Creepscreech's lair." She looked about her, a frown wrinkling her brow.

"Wait a minute," Mouse exclaimed. "There's lots of the Rhymer's papers here."

"Papers?" inquired Podge. "'Pon my... At a time like this you want us to read poems?"

"No," said Mouse. "But if we set fire to them, how would that be?"

"I certainly don't want to read a poem that's on fire." Podge sounded annoyed.

Then he understood. "Oh, yes, I see now. You mean..."

"Torches!" cried Alkus. "Good idea, Mouse." She picked up several sheets of discarded paper and twisted them tightly together. Everyone followed her example and, working in hectic silence, they produced a good armful of torches in a short time. Alkus lit one and handed the blazing beacon to the groundhog. "You first, Chuck," she said. The groundhog nodded stoically and, holding the flaming torch before him, wriggled on his stomach headfirst into the mole-sized hole in the ground. "Now you, Qwolsh. Be ready to grab his ankle so he doesn't fall through. I'll be ready to grab yours."

As Qwolsh disappeared on hands and knees on the heels of the groundhog, Alkus said to Mouse, "Obviously you won't get much more than your arms in, but if you reach down as far as you can and hold my ankles, you can be the anchor. Podge, you get busy twisting more papers together." So saying, she stuffed a bundle

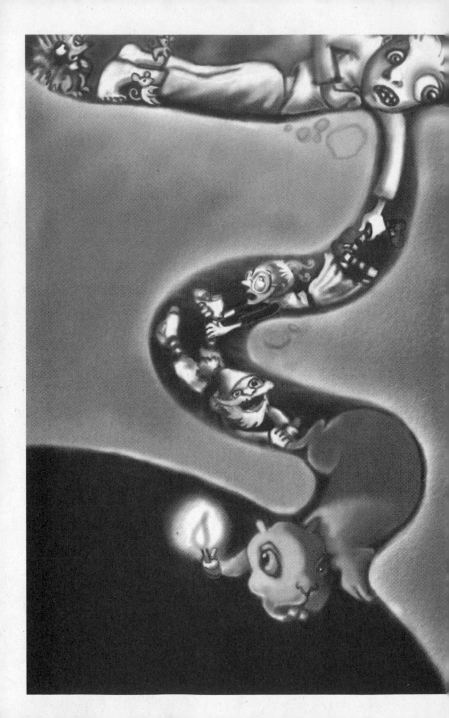

of unlit torches into her belt and crawled into the hole after Qwolsh.

Mouse lay full length on the ground and reached an arm into the hole until he seized Alkus's ankle. He felt something at his own ankles: Snick and Snock had grabbed a pajama leg each and were holding on for all they were worth. Initially smoke from Chuck's torch drifted backward, irritating Mouse's nostrils, but it stopped as the torch entered the Creepscreech's tunnel below.

In the distance they heard the faraway voice of the groundhog. "It's a tunnel all right, and it's huge," he called. "Huge-huge-huge," his voice came reverberating back.

"Can you see anything?" shouted Alkus.

"I think there's water on the ground far below," called the groundhog. "Below-below-below," replied the echo. "I can't see any walls from here; it's very black. And it's cold."

"Cold-cold-cold," agreed the tunnel.

"I think I can hear...Agh! Pull me up, pull me up. Quick! Quick! Hurry up! Quick! Quickquickquick!" All of this came out in such a rush that it ran together with its echoes as, from far off, the rapidly rising roar of the Creepscreech reached Mouse's ears.

He scrambled backward as fast as he could, pulling Alkus and knocking the deer mice flying in the process. As soon as Alkus's feet came into view, Mouse reached past her, grabbed hold of Qwolsh and pulled. But before Qwolsh's legs were even out of the hole, a gibbering, chattering Chuck appeared. Somehow he had managed to turn around and scamper up across Qwolsh's back. A pained bellow from Qwolsh was drowned out by the Creepscreech's roar. Scrambling rapidly away from the edge of the hole, they ended up in a jumbled pile, a tangle of arms and tails and legs and paws. They lay like that, hushed and holding on to each other, long after the roar of the Creepscreech had subsided.

Finally Chuck broke the silence. "It was horrible," he sobbed. "An icy blast hit me and when I looked I could see its evil yellow eyes rushing at me. It almost... oh!" He was nearly overcome at this point but managed to go on. "It almost grabbed me. Ugh! It was big, and shiny with slime. Horrible!"

Qwolsh cleared his throat. "No...er...sign of Digger?" he asked hesitantly. Chuck squinted at Qwolsh with sorrow-filled eyes. He blinked once and looked down-ward, shaking his head slowly from side to side. The blinking became more rapid, as though he had something in his eye. Which indeed he had. Mouse saw a big teardrop well up from within, tremble in the corner of the groundhog's eye for a moment, then break free and roll down his snout to plop onto the ground below, making a small crater in the dust.

All the Undergardeners, in fact, were close to tears. The deer mice were so heartsick that when Snick, or maybe it was Snock, said, "Poor Digger," Snock

97

(or Snick) didn't join in, just gave a deep sigh.

Mouse himself was greatly upset, but he was determined not to let down his newfound friends. Some attempt, no matter how futile, had to be made to save the mole. "We can't just give up," he said. "We have to get down into that tunnel."

"Down?" Shock was evident in the groundhog's voice. "You want to go down into the Creepscreech's lair?"

"You don't want to leave Digger down there alone, do you?" asked Mouse. "Especially if there's still a chance to save him."

"No! No, we don't, Mouse," said Alkus firmly. "You're right." She collected the mole's scattered spectacles and turned to the others. "We have to do something. We can't just leave him. Not as long as we have breath in our bodies."

"Breath in our bodies," echoed Qwolsh forcefully, and the others took it up as a rallying cry. "Breath in our bodies!" they shouted determinedly, and the tunnel about them rang with their voices.

"Well, it will be difficult. The Creep-screech's lair is very high," said Chuck. "We'll need lots of rope, and we'll be very exposed on the climb down. Extremely dangerous!"

"Besides," interjected Podge, "Mouse here would never get through that tunnel Digger just made." He sounded reluctant to go without Mouse.

"Wait a minute," said Mouse to Podge. "What about that larder you told us about? The one you were digging when you broke through. Could we get through that way?"

"Plugged it, didn't I?" said Podge.

"Could we unplug it?" Qwolsh wanted to know.

"Well, yes, I suppose so." Podge nodded doubtfully.

"Show us where it is," said Mouse decisively.

"Follow me, then." Podge spun around and set off down the main tunnel; the others—an uneasy mix of determination and trepidation—followed his twitching quills. The farther they went, the lower the tunnel became, and Mouse had to walk bent over, but at last they got to a section of wall that was stoutly boarded over with crude planks.

"Here we are," said Podge, slapping the barrier.

Alkus stood back to assess the job. "You did a good job here, Podge." She paused and Podge smiled with pride. "I'm sorry to say," she finished and Podge's smile faded. "It'll take a while to shift this. Right, let's get to it." They all set to with a will. Using hammers and bars and axes from their tool bags, they began to pound and pry and lever at the planks.

Chapter 9

After much pulling and prying and levering and grunting, Mouse and the others had cleared away the barrier that closed off Podge's old pantry and in they went, Mouse's head scraping the roof. A cold breeze blew from a hole in the opposite wall, the hole where Podge had broken through into the Creepscreech's lair. They set to again, clawing and digging and scooping away sufficient earth to make the hole big enough to crawl through.

For the journey ahead, the Undergardeners had collected handheld lanterns and a coil of rope; some of their larger tools would come in handy as weapons. For his own protection, Mouse selected a hefty length of wood from Podge's barricade. He hoped he wouldn't get an opportunity to test it, but just having it made him feel safer. At intervals along the rope, Alkus made loops for each of them to put an arm through. "Don't want anyone to get lost," she said. "I want us linked together all the time we're in there. Now, a quick roll call. Snick and Snock."

"Here," the deer mice answered, for once in unison. Stepping smartly forward they saluted together, one with the left arm, the other with the right.

Alkus made a mark on the clipboard and called, "Chuck!"

"That's me," answered the groundhog, waddling forward.

"Yes, I know it's you." Alkus sounded irritated. "Please answer in the approved fashion."

"Oh, pardon me," said Chuck haughtily. "He-re!"

"That's better," said Alkus. "Podge!"

"Hummh?" mumbled Podge, pulling his head in from the opening into the Creepscreech's lair.

"Please answer when I call your name," said Alkus.

"My name? Why, Podge!" Podge sounded puzzled.

"This is a roll call," explained Alkus patiently. "Podge!"

"Yes?" said Podge.

"Here," shouted Alkus.

"Where?" said Podge, giving a startled jump.

Mouse intervened. "She wants you to answer 'Here' when she calls your name."

"Does she, by gollopers?" Podge looked at Alkus. Then he looked back at Mouse. "Why didn't she say so? Tell her—here." He moved into the line as Alkus muttered to herself.

"Qwolsh!" she continued.

"Here," said Qwolsh, taking his place.

And "Here," said Mouse, stepping into the line as his own name was called.

Alkus placed herself in front of Mouse, who could see the logic in this arrangement. Snick and Snock, the smallest, were at the front; the tallest, Mouse, was at the back; the others were graded in between according to height. This way, each could see over the heads of those in front and had a clear view of whatever danger might lie ahead.

The lanterns were lit. As though on cue, each took a deep breath at the same time. Mouse pulled his pajama top tighter around him, set his shoulders and took a firm grip on his wooden cudgel. Somebody said, quietly and determinedly, "Breath in our bodies." All took up the call. "Breath in our bodies!" they whispered fiercely as they moved toward the dreaded hole.

Although Snick and Snock were in front, they weren't so much leading as being pushed. Chuck gave them a boost with an upward swing of his snout. Leaping forward with a shared "Oof," they disappeared into the dark on the end of the taut rope.

The tunnel was quite small, not nearly as large as the tunnel that Digger had fallen into, so they decided this was most likely a ventilation shaft—or perhaps a drain, for it seemed damp. Far off in the distance, the tiniest glimmer of bluish light showed, and with Snick and Snock reluctantly leading the way, they headed in that direction, their flickering lanterns casting madly dancing shadows in the gloom about them as they went.

Reaching up, Mouse could just touch the curve of the roof; under his bare feet was a coating of something that felt damp and vaguely slimy, and there was a musty odor in the air. As the sickly blue light drew nearer, the deer mice became even more reluctant to lead and dawdled and drifted from side to side. "Get a move on, you two," urged Chuck when they had got under his feet for the umpteenth time.

"Wouldn't you...

...rather go...

...first?" they wanted to know.

"Scared, eh?" muttered Chuck.

105

"Not...

...at all," they said. They paused briefly and looked at one another. Then they chipped in again. "Tired...

We're tired, that's...

...all!" They yawned and let their heads hang as though they were so exhausted they could no longer hold them upright.

"Want me to carry you?" Mouse asked.

"Oh, yes...

...please, Mouse...

...Mountain. Whee...

...eee!" They ran back toward Mouse, all thoughts of looking tired forgotten. They also forgot that they were looped together by the rope and ran one each side of Chuck, tripping him.

"Agh!" The sound was driven from the groundhog as he toppled to the ground. By the time he had grumbled himself back onto his feet, Snick and Snock were snugly standing in the breast pocket of Mouse's pajamas, looking like happy passengers at a ship's rail.

Then they all heard it. From the direction of the light came the sullen rumble of a disturbed beast. "Let me go first," said Mouse. No sooner had he said it than the deer mice lost all interest in their new mode of transport and were seized by a sudden urge to walk again. Scurrying down to the ground, they moved unobtrusively to the back. The lanterns were extinguished and, heart pounding and clutching the cudgel, Mouse edged slowly forward, going on hands and knees for the last few yards.

The sound was much nearer now and getting louder every second. The odd thing was, it seemed vaguely familiar to Mouse. His head came out slowly into the Creepscreech's lair, and right before his horrified eyes was a pool of what looked like blood. We're too late, was the thought that flashed through his mind before the lights suddenly went out. From the darkness came a grating squeal and then... silence.

Mouse drew back instantly. "I think,"

he whispered, "we may have set off an alarm of some sort. Don't move." They huddled close and listened. Not a sound came from the tunnel. Cautiously Mouse eased his head out for another look. Blackness. Not total, though, because as his eyes grew accustomed to the gloom, he saw faint light in the distance. A silvery shimmer on the ground in places suggested watery pools. Water dripped monotonously in the cavern. *Drip. Drip. Drip.* Each drip was followed by its ghostly echo. *Dri...pip. Dri...pip. Dri...pip.*

Then there came a distinct cackle of laughter and they heard a voice say, "Ah-ha! From his tail I have taken the sting."

"That sounds like..." began Alkus.

"...Digger, by gollopers!" finished Podge, in Snick and Snock fashion.

"I'll go and check," said Chuck, drawing breath past his bared teeth.

"All right," said Alkus, "but hold on to the end of the rope."

The groundhog set off with the rope end between his teeth, Alkus paying out the slack behind him as he went. The animal's rotund form quickly disappeared into the gloom. They waited in silence, eyes straining into the darkness. The coil of rope in Alkus's hands got smaller and smaller and had almost run out completely when they heard a cry and a thud from the darkness as though someone had been hit.

"Take that, you monster!" It *was* Digger. Stifling a desire to cry out with joy, they all ran quietly forward, stumbling over each other in their haste.

"Why did you—*ow!*—hit me?" came Chuck's pained voice.

"Chuck? Sorry, Chuck, didn't know it was you. Expecting the Creepscreech I was." Digger was all apologies. "Who's that?" he suddenly asked the darkness anxiously.

"It's only us," said Alkus, lighting a lantern. The sudden flare of light hurt their eyes for a second; then they got a good look at a disheveled and bloodied but still feisty Digger, and at poor Chuck, who was tenderly feeling his punched snout and knuckling tears away from his eyes.

Forgetting the danger they were in, they gathered in a circle around Digger and all began talking at the same time. What happened? Did the Creepscreech bite you? How big is it? Where is it now? Did you fight it off? Poor Digger was almost ashamed to admit that he hadn't been close to the Creepscreech at all, that he had only seen its eyes in the distance and that the cut on his head wasn't a bite from the creature's terrible fangs.

"I gashed it when the ground I hit," said the mole, feeling the top of his head gingerly. "It seems now to have stopped bleeding. I called and called but only an echo replied. And then the monster thundered around the bend. Oh, I was sure I was done for. In the dark I felt something sticking from the wall. I grabbed it and pulled, thinking it was something I could as a weapon use, but all just went black and I was covered with shooting stars. The Creepscreech went silent, but I did not know if it had stopped or was maybe sliddering toward me in the dark." Digger shuddered as he recalled the fear and despair he had felt at finding himself alone in this awful place. "That was why I punched you. I thought maybe you were it." He looked apologetically at Chuck, who was gently massaging the end of his muzzle.

They were all delighted to see Digger safe and sound and began bombarding him with questions, but Alkus decided it would be better to continue the discussion in the safety of one of their own tunnels and began hustling them back the way they had come.

Meanwhile Mouse was examining this tunnel. He felt the smoothness of the walls. It wasn't earth; it was...stone. This Creepscreech must be quite a brute if it could chew through stone. He didn't have much time to puzzle about it, however, because coming toward them, cutting off their retreat, was a cluster of dancing lights.

Alkus quickly blew out the lantern and they huddled together in the dark. As the lights came nearer, Mouse and the Undergardeners retreated as silently as they could. Back over the sharp stones they went. Back past where Digger had been knocked flat by a shower of stars. Mouse stumbled and, putting out his hands to steady himself, found what he thought was an opening to another tunnel. He pulled everyone in, but to his horror the opening didn't lead any-where—it was just a little alcove a few feet deep. It was too late to escape because now the lights were close, clustered around where Digger had seen the shooting stars.

"Here's the problem," said a voice.

"The switch is open," said another.

There was a clunk, a few sparks, and pale blue lights lit the tunnel. There was a squeal and the eyes of the Creepscreech opened and began to move closer. The Undergardeners shivered with fear.

"It's coming," they chattered.

"It's seen us," they cried.

"We're done for," they whimpered.

"What'll we do, Mouse?" they pleaded.

Mouse began to laugh. A quiet chuckle at first, which grew in volume as the monster thundered toward them. It became louder as it got closer, gathering speed as it came. Then it screeched past in a swirling blast of cold air and dust. The dust got in his throat and stopped Mouse's laughter briefly, but after a couple of coughs, he started again. All the Undergardeners were clinging to him—and one another—with their eyes tightly closed. Alkus was the first to open hers. She glared at Mouse. "Have you gone... why are you laughing?"

"We're in a tunnel. A train tunnel," Mouse managed to gasp. "The Creepscreech is a train. Look, there are the tracks."

The three workers who had closed the big electricity switch were walking away

from them between the tracks with flash-lights in their hands. Two men and one woman. Three ordinary-looking workers in yellow hard hats and work clothes.

Mouse explained what a train was and told them that sometimes trains went through tunnels like this one. "Digger must have pulled the main switch and cut off the power; that's why it stopped. But we should get out in case any more trains come because even though it's not the monster you thought it was, it's still dangerous. Apart from the possibility of getting run over, that rail," he pointed, "carries the electricity that powers the train. It can kill. Now, let me see. We don't have to go back the way we came; we can go this way. I can see moonlight."

Alkus relit her lantern and made a note on her clipboard. *Send a work crew to fill in the hole outside the Ancient Rhymer's cave before it causes more trouble. And seal Podge's pantry again.*

As the grateful Undergardeners thanked Mouse for revealing what the

Creepscreech really was, he found out how the myth had come into being. Back when the tunnel was being built, some of the Undergardeners in those olden times had been killed in the blasting. The generations of Undergardeners that came after never went near the tunnel again, and the myth of the monstrous Creepscreech grew and grew. Digger shook his head ruefully. "Fear has a big shadow," he said, "but he himself is very small."

Podge drew himself up on his hind legs and shook himself gleefully, his own spiky shadow looking huge and menacing in the light from the lantern. "You did a splendid night's work, Mouse," he said, his monocle glinting. "By gollopers, yes. You're a hero."

Everyone agreed cheerfully, and Mouse felt proud. A hero, by gollopers, he thought as he led the happy Undergardeners along the tunnel toward the circle of light he knew was the night sky. They streamed out into the moon-bright, open-to-the-sky, outside world.

Chapter 10

Mouse took a deep breath of the night air. Being below ground with the Undergardeners had been wonderful, but fresh air and moonlight and space were nice too. Looking around, he was surprised to recognize his surroundings. While underground he had felt he was a thousand miles away, yet here he was at a railway bridge not very far from his own home. The river flowing under the bridge ran through the park at the back of his house; a fast walk and he could be home in minutes. Mouse had never seen the park at this hour: dark, shadowy, moody, mysterious and silent, except for the flowing river whispering to the rocks.

Sooner than he wanted, they came within sight of his back garden and the fenceposts he and his father had erected. In the moonlight they looked like small, square, branchless trees. The house was in darkness, which meant he hadn't been missed; Mouse could sneak back to bed and nobody would be the wiser. But, tired though he was, he didn't *want* to go to bed, didn't want the evening to end. "Can we meet again?" he asked, looking beseechingly at Alkus.

Alkus looked up at Mouse and then turned to the others. All nodded their agreement without hesitation. "It seems to be unanimous," she said with a smile. "Let's sole on it." One after the other they all solemnly touched toes with Mouse. "Now remember, Mouse," Alkus continued, "this has to be our secret. We can't have Uptoppers interfering with our lives, which they would if they found out about us. Promise?" Mouse nodded vigorously.

At the edge of the hole where the adventure had started, the Undergardeners hummed the rock into its open position. Suddenly Mouse had an awful thought. "But if we fill in this hole," he said, "you won't be able to raise the rock!"

"Oh, that's all right," exclaimed Alkus. "We have lots of entrances. Hollow trees, the edge of the riverbank, under other rocks—we have many ways in and out. In fact, until tonight, this portal hadn't been used since before these houses and gardens were built." She gestured about her with both hands. "Thank you for everything, Mouse. Next time we're working near here we'll get a message to you and we'll meet again."

With one last goodbye to them all, Mouse turned and headed toward his back door.

Back in his bedroom, he knew he should try to wash away all trace of the Undergarden, but he was afraid that the noise would wake his parents. That was his excuse, anyway. Let his mother wonder tomorrow how he managed to get muddy while he slept. Exhausted, he climbed into bed, his mind still buzzing with excitement. He was pleased with himself too. If I hadn't rushed out to help Qwolsh, look what I would have missed—the best adventure I've ever had in my life. I'm a hero, by gollopers.

And with that happy thought, Mouse fell into a deep and dreamless sleep.

photo credit: Trevor Black

Desmond Anthony Ellis lives in a house in Toronto that backs onto a park full of animals. There's a river and a railway bridge nearby and lots of hiding places among trees and bushes; the perfect place for a boy to grow up. A place very like where Mouse lives, in fact. *The Undergardeners* is his first book.